D1072664

Silly Stories

How the Leopard Got His Spots

and Other Silly Stories

Compiled by Vic Parker

Gareth Stevens
PUBLISHING

Please visit our website, **www.garethstevens.com**.
For a free color catalog of all our high-quality books,
call toll free 1-800-542-2595 or fax 1-877-542-2596.

Cataloging-in-Publication Data
Parker, Vic.
How the leopard got his spots and other silly stories / by Vic Parker.
p. cm. — (Silly stories)
Includes index.
ISBN 978-1-4824-4191-8 (pbk.)
ISBN 978-1-4824-4192-5 (6 pack)
ISBN 978-1-4824-4193-2 (library binding)
1. Children's stories. 2. Humorous stories.
I. Parker, Victoria. II. Title.
PZ8.P35 Ho 2016
398.2—d23

Published in 2016 by
Gareth Stevens Publishing
111 East 14th Street, Suite 349
New York, NY 10003

Publishing Director | Belinda Gallagher
Creative Director | Jo Cowan
Editorial Director | Rosie McGuire
Senior Editor | Carly Blake
Editorial Assistant | Amy Johnson
Designer | Joe Jones
Production Manager | Elizabeth Collins
Reprographics | Stephan Davis, Jennifer Hunt, Thom Allaway

Acknowlegments
The publishers would like to thank the following artists who have
contributed to this book:
Beehive Illustration Agency: Rosie Brooks, Mike Phillips (inc. cover)
Lisa Bentley, Aimee Mappley (decorative frames)
All other artwork from the Miles Kelly Artwork Bank

Printed in the United States of America
CPSIA compliance information: Batch # CW16GS:
For further information contact Gareth Stevens, New York, New York at 1-800-542-2595.

Contents

The Four Little Children Who Went Round the World

By Edward Lear

Once upon a time, a long while ago, there were four little children whose names were Violet, Slingsby, Guy, and Lionel, and they all thought they should like to see the world. So they bought a large boat to sail round the world by sea, planning to come back on the other side by land. The boat was painted blue with green spots, and the

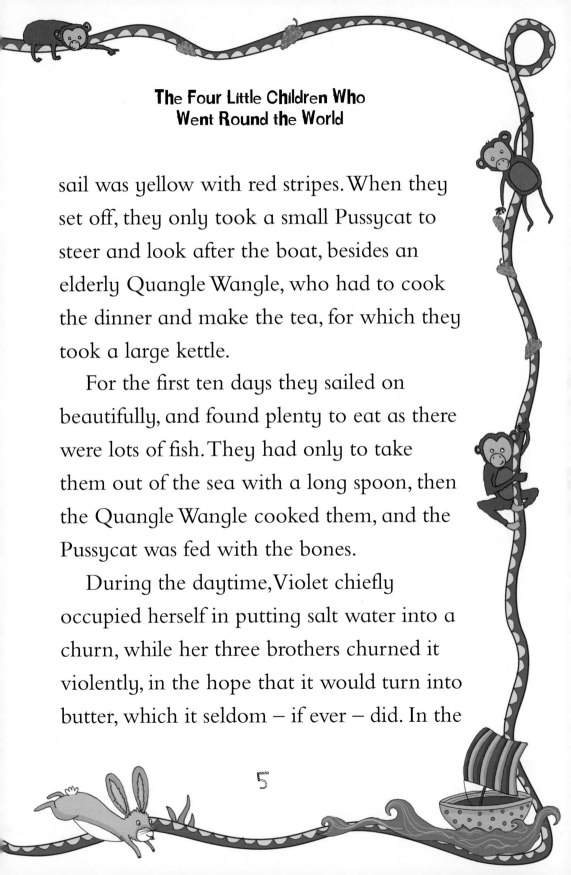

The Four Little Children Who Went Round the World

sail was yellow with red stripes. When they set off, they only took a small Pussycat to steer and look after the boat, besides an elderly Quangle Wangle, who had to cook the dinner and make the tea, for which they took a large kettle.

For the first ten days they sailed on beautifully, and found plenty to eat as there were lots of fish. They had only to take them out of the sea with a long spoon, then the Quangle Wangle cooked them, and the Pussycat was fed with the bones.

During the daytime, Violet chiefly occupied herself in putting salt water into a churn, while her three brothers churned it violently, in the hope that it would turn into butter, which it seldom – if ever – did. In the

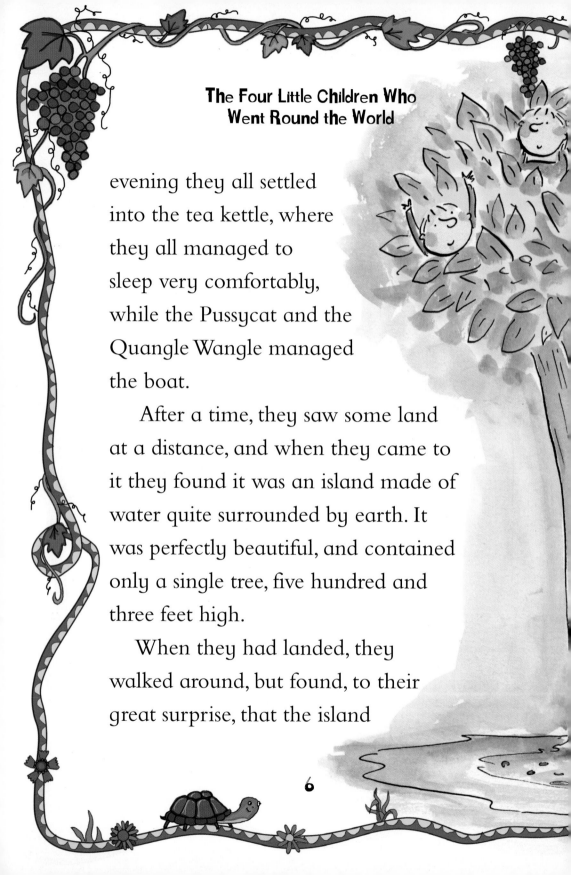

evening they all settled
into the tea kettle, where
they all managed to
sleep very comfortably,
while the Pussycat and the
Quangle Wangle managed
the boat.

　　After a time, they saw some land
at a distance, and when they came to
it they found it was an island made of
water quite surrounded by earth. It
was perfectly beautiful, and contained
only a single tree, five hundred and
three feet high.

　　When they had landed, they
walked around, but found, to their
great surprise, that the island

The Four Little Children Who Went Round the World

was quite full of veal cutlets and chocolate drops, and nothing else. So they all climbed up the single high tree to discover, if possible, if there were any people. Having remained on the top of the tree for a week, and not seeing anybody, they concluded that there were no inhabitants. When they came down, they loaded the boat with two thousand veal cutlets and a million chocolate drops, and these kept them going for more than a month as they voyaged onward.

The Four Little Children Who Went Round the World

After this they came to a shore where there were no less than sixty-five great red parrots with blue tails, sitting on a rail in a row, and all fast asleep. And I am sorry to say that the Pussycat and the Quangle Wangle crept softly, and bit off the tail feathers of all the sixty-five parrots. Violet stuck two hundred and sixty of the feathers in her bonnet, so it looked lovely and glittering.

Next, they came to a narrow part of the sea which was so entirely full of fish that the boat could go on no farther: so they remained there about six weeks, feasting on them. Many of the uneaten fish complained of the cold, as well as

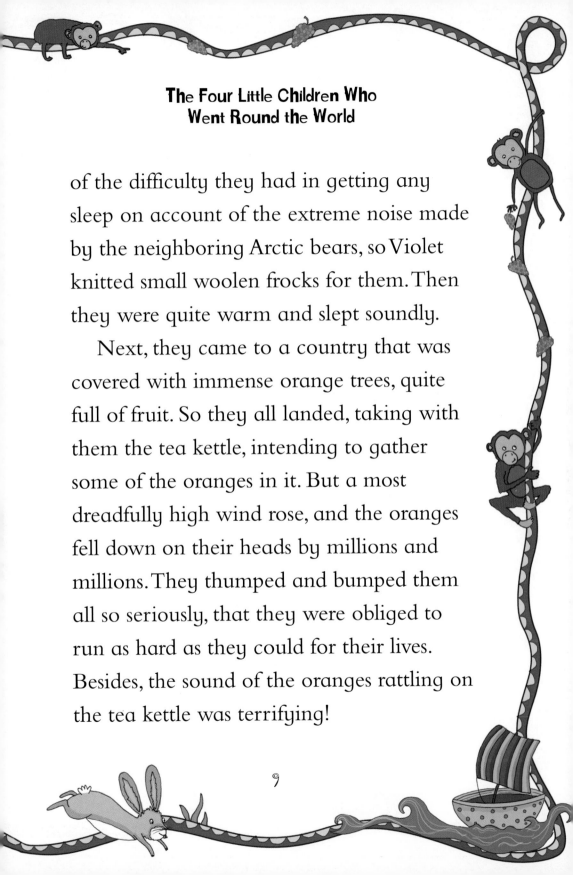

of the difficulty they had in getting any sleep on account of the extreme noise made by the neighboring Arctic bears, so Violet knitted small woolen frocks for them. Then they were quite warm and slept soundly.

Next, they came to a country that was covered with immense orange trees, quite full of fruit. So they all landed, taking with them the tea kettle, intending to gather some of the oranges in it. But a most dreadfully high wind rose, and the oranges fell down on their heads by millions and millions. They thumped and bumped them all so seriously, that they were obliged to run as hard as they could for their lives. Besides, the sound of the oranges rattling on the tea kettle was terrifying!

The Four Little Children Who Went Round the World

They got safely to the boat and, after sailing on calmly for several more days, they came to another country, where they were pleased and surprised to see countless white Mice with red eyes, all sitting in a great circle, slowly eating custard pudding.

As the four travelers were rather hungry, tired of eating fish and oranges for so long a period, Guy asked the Mice for some of their pudding. But no sooner had he finished talking than the Mice turned round and sneezed at him! At this scroobious sound Guy rushed back to the boat.

By and by the four children came to a vast, wide plain, on which nothing could be discovered at first. As the travelers walked on there appeared in the distance an object,

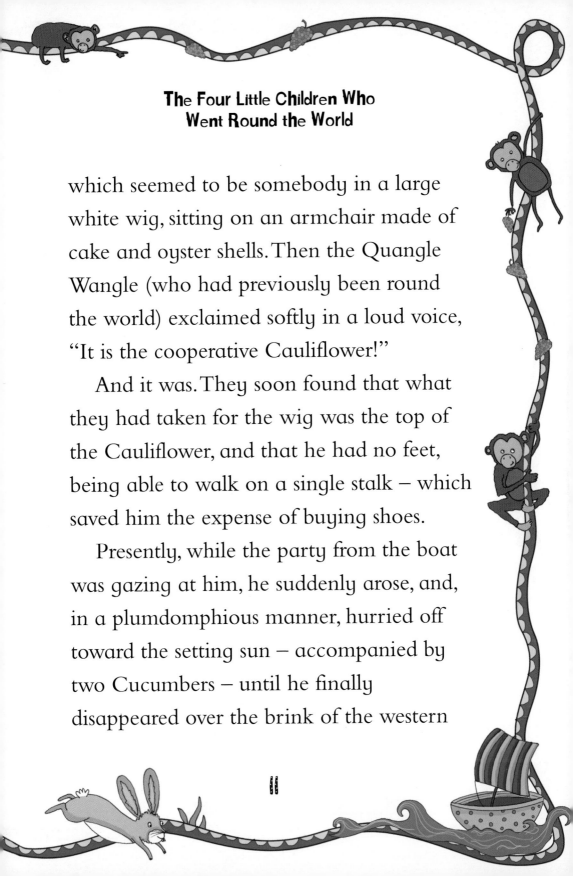

The Four Little Children Who
Went Round the World

which seemed to be somebody in a large
white wig, sitting on an armchair made of
cake and oyster shells. Then the Quangle
Wangle (who had previously been round
the world) exclaimed softly in a loud voice,
"It is the cooperative Cauliflower!"

And it was. They soon found that what
they had taken for the wig was the top of
the Cauliflower, and that he had no feet,
being able to walk on a single stalk – which
saved him the expense of buying shoes.

Presently, while the party from the boat
was gazing at him, he suddenly arose, and,
in a plumdomphious manner, hurried off
toward the setting sun – accompanied by
two Cucumbers – until he finally
disappeared over the brink of the western

sky.

Shortly after, the travelers sailed below some high overhanging rocks, from the top of which a little boy dressed in rose-colored knickerbockers threw an enormous pumpkin at the boat, which hit it and overturned it! Luckily all the party knew how to swim, and they paddled about until after the moon rose, when they righted the boat and boarded it once again.

Two or three days afterward, they came to a place where they found nothing at all except some wide and deep pits full of mulberry jam. This was the property of tiny, yellow-nosed Apes who store up the mulberry jam for their food in winter, when they mix it with pale periwinkle soup, and serve it out in china bowls, which grow

freely all over
that part of the
country. Only one
of the yellow-nosed
Apes was on the spot and he was fast asleep,
yet the four travelers, the Quangle Wangle
and Pussycat were so terrified by the sound
of his snoring they merely took a small
cupful of the jam and returned to their boat
without delay.

What was their horror on seeing the
boat in the mouth of an enormous Seeze

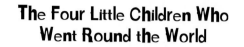

Pyder, a ferocious creature truly dreadful to
behold! In a moment, the beautiful boat
was bitten into fifty-five thousand million
hundred billion bits. It became quite clear
that Violet, Slingsby, Guy, and Lionel could
no longer carry on their voyage by sea.

The four travelers had to make their way
on land. Fortunately, there happened to pass
by an elderly Rhinoceros, on which they
seized, and, all four mounting on his back –
the Quangle Wangle sitting on his horn,
and the Pussycat swinging at the end of his
tail – they set off, having only four small
beans and three pounds of mashed potatoes
to last them.

They were, however, able to catch
numbers of the chickens, turkeys, and other

birds who continually landed on the head
of the Rhinoceros to gather the seeds of the
rhododendron plants which grew there. A
crowd of Kangaroos and gigantic Cranes
accompanied them, and they went onward
in a triumphant procession.

In less than eighteen weeks they all arrived
safely home, where they were received by
their admiring relatives with joy.

How the Leopard Got His Spots

By Rudyard Kipling

Long, long ago, the Leopard lived in the 'sclusively bare, hot, shiny High Veldt, where there was sand and sandy-colored rock and 'sclusively tufts of sandy-yellowish grass. The Giraffe, the Zebra, the Eland, the Kudu, and the Hartebeest lived there, and they were 'sclusively sandy-yellow-brownish all over.

But the Leopard, he was the 'sclusivest
sandiest-yellowish-brownest of them all –
a grayish-yellowish catty-
shaped beast, and he
matched the 'sclusively
yellowish-grayish-brown of
the High Veldt to one hair.
This was very bad
for the Giraffe, the
Zebra, and the rest of them, for
he would lie down by a
'sclusively yellowish-grayish-brownish stone
or clump of grass, and when the Giraffe,
the Zebra, the Eland, the Kudu,
the Bushbuck, or the Bontebok came
by he would surprise them out of their
jumpsome lives!

How the Leopard Got His Spots

There was an Ethiopian with bows and arrows (a 'sclusively grayish-brownish-yellowish man he was then), who lived on the High Veldt with the Leopard. The two used to hunt together – the Ethiopian with his bows and arrows, and the Leopard 'sclusively with his teeth and claws – till the Giraffe, the Eland, the Kudu, the Quagga, and all the rest of them didn't know which way to jump!

After a long time, the animals learned to avoid anything that looked like a Leopard or an Ethiopian, and bit by bit – the Giraffe began it, because his legs were the longest – they went away from the High Veldt.

They scuttled for days and days and days till they came to a great forest, 'sclusively full of trees and bushes and stripy, speckly, patchy-blatchy shadows, and there they hid. After another long time, what with standing half in the shade and half out of it, and what with the slippery-slidy shadows of the trees falling on them, the Giraffe grew blotchy, and the Zebra grew stripy, and the Eland and the Kudu grew darker, with little wavy gray lines on their backs like bark on a tree trunk. And so, though you could hear them and smell them, you could very seldom see them, and then only when you knew precisely where to look.

They had a beautiful time in the 'sclusively speckly-spickly shadows of the forest. Meanwhile, the Leopard and the Ethiopian ran about over the 'sclusively grayish-yellowish-reddish High Veldt outside, wondering where their breakfasts and their dinners and their teas had gone.

At last they were so hungry that they ate rats, beetles, and rock-rabbits, the Leopard and the Ethiopian, and then they both had the big tummy-ache. Then they met Baviaan – the dog-headed, barking Baboon, who is quite the wisest animal in all South Africa.

Said Leopard to Baviaan, "Where has all the game gone?"

Then said Baviaan, "The game has gone

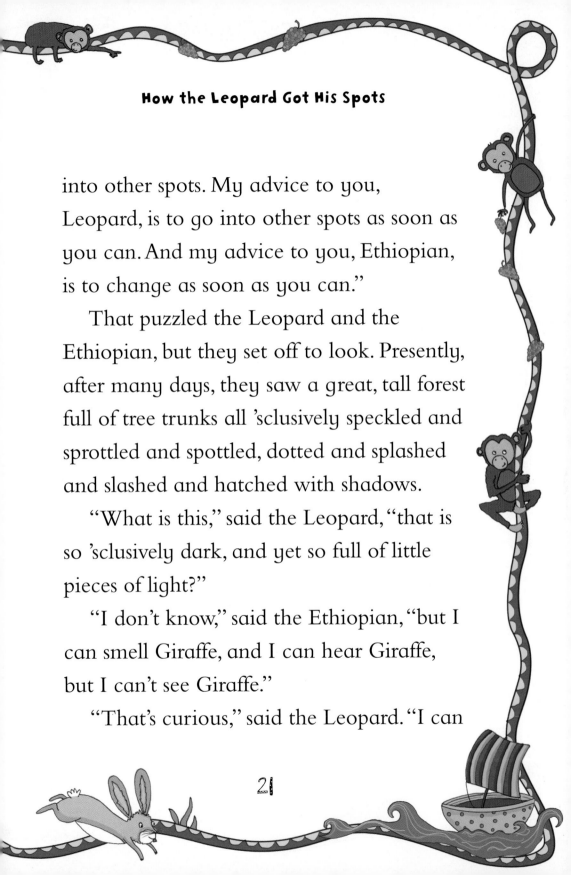

into other spots. My advice to you,
Leopard, is to go into other spots as soon as
you can. And my advice to you, Ethiopian,
is to change as soon as you can."

That puzzled the Leopard and the
Ethiopian, but they set off to look. Presently,
after many days, they saw a great, tall forest
full of tree trunks all 'sclusively speckled and
sprottled and spottled, dotted and splashed
and slashed and hatched with shadows.

"What is this," said the Leopard, "that is
so 'sclusively dark, and yet so full of little
pieces of light?"

"I don't know," said the Ethiopian, "but I
can smell Giraffe, and I can hear Giraffe,
but I can't see Giraffe."

"That's curious," said the Leopard. "I can

smell Zebra, and I can hear Zebra, but I can't see Zebra."

"Wait a bit," said the Ethiopian. "Perhaps we've forgotten what they were like."

"I remember them perfectly on the High Veldt," said the Leopard. "Giraffe is about seventeen feet high, of a 'sclusively golden-yellow. Zebra is about four and a half feet high, of a 'sclusively gray-fawn color."

The Leopard and the Ethiopian hunted all day, and though they could smell them and hear them, they never saw one of them.

So they waited till dark, and then the Leopard heard something breathing sniffily in the starlight that fell all stripy through the branches. He jumped at the noise. It smelled like Zebra, and it felt like Zebra, and when he knocked it down it kicked like Zebra, but he couldn't see it. So he said, "Be quiet, O you person without any form. I am going to sit on your head until morning, because there is something about you that I don't understand."

Then he heard a grunt and a crash, and the Ethiopian called out, "I've caught a thing that I can't see. It smells like Giraffe, and kicks like Giraffe, but it hasn't any form."

"Don't you trust it," said the Leopard. "Sit on its head until the morning, same as me. They haven't any form – any of 'em."

So they sat down on them hard until bright morning time, and then Leopard said, "What have you at your end of the table, Brother?"

How the Leopard Got His Spots

The Ethiopian scratched his head and said, "It ought to be Giraffe, but it is covered all over with chestnut blotches. What have you at your end of the table, Brother?"

The Leopard scratched his head and said, "It ought to be Zebra, but it is covered all over with black and gray stripes. What have you been doing to yourself, Zebra? Don't you know that if you were on the

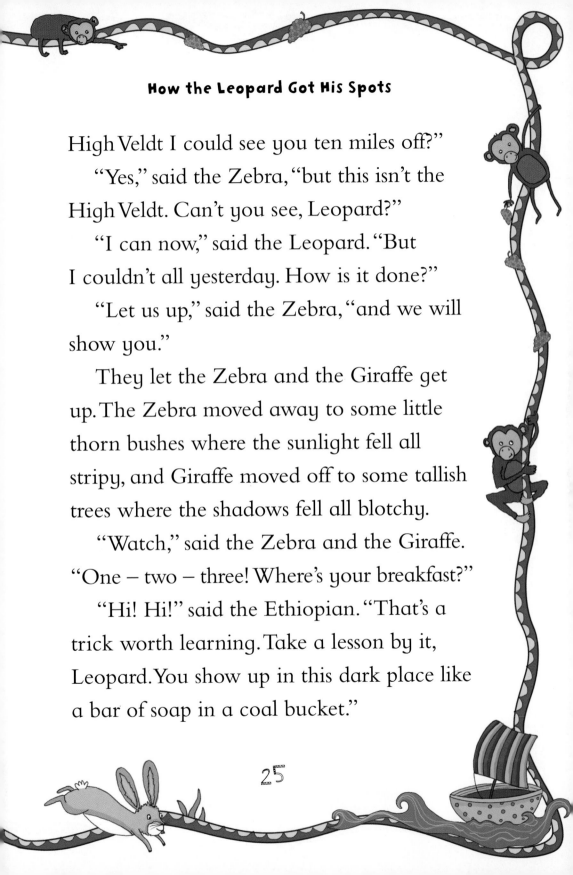

High Veldt I could see you ten miles off?"

"Yes," said the Zebra, "but this isn't the High Veldt. Can't you see, Leopard?"

"I can now," said the Leopard. "But I couldn't all yesterday. How is it done?"

"Let us up," said the Zebra, "and we will show you."

They let the Zebra and the Giraffe get up. The Zebra moved away to some little thorn bushes where the sunlight fell all stripy, and Giraffe moved off to some tallish trees where the shadows fell all blotchy.

"Watch," said the Zebra and the Giraffe. "One – two – three! Where's your breakfast?"

"Hi! Hi!" said the Ethiopian. "That's a trick worth learning. Take a lesson by it, Leopard. You show up in this dark place like a bar of soap in a coal bucket."

"Ho! Ho!" said the Leopard. "You show up in this dark place like a mustard plaster on a sack of coals."

"Well, calling names won't catch dinner," said the Ethiopian. "Baviaan's told me I ought to change. As I've nothing to change except my skin, I'm going to change that."

"What to?" said the Leopard, excited.

"To a nice working blackish-brownish color, with a little purple in it, and touches of slate-blue. It will be the very thing for hiding in hollows and behind trees."

He changed his skin then and there, and the Leopard was more excited than ever – he had never seen a man change his skin.

"But what about me?" the Leopard said.

"You take Baviaan's advice too. He told

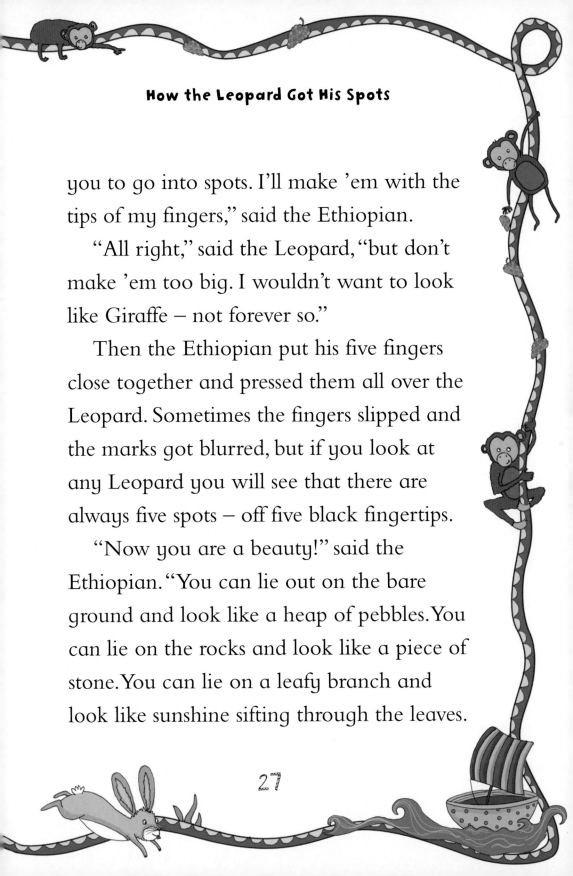

you to go into spots. I'll make 'em with the tips of my fingers," said the Ethiopian.

"All right," said the Leopard, "but don't make 'em too big. I wouldn't want to look like Giraffe – not forever so."

Then the Ethiopian put his five fingers close together and pressed them all over the Leopard. Sometimes the fingers slipped and the marks got blurred, but if you look at any Leopard you will see that there are always five spots – off five black fingertips.

"Now you are a beauty!" said the Ethiopian. "You can lie out on the bare ground and look like a heap of pebbles. You can lie on the rocks and look like a piece of stone. You can lie on a leafy branch and look like sunshine sifting through the leaves.

Now, we'll see
if we can't get even with
Mr. One–Two–Three Where's
your Breakfast!"
So they went away and lived
happily ever afterward. That is all.

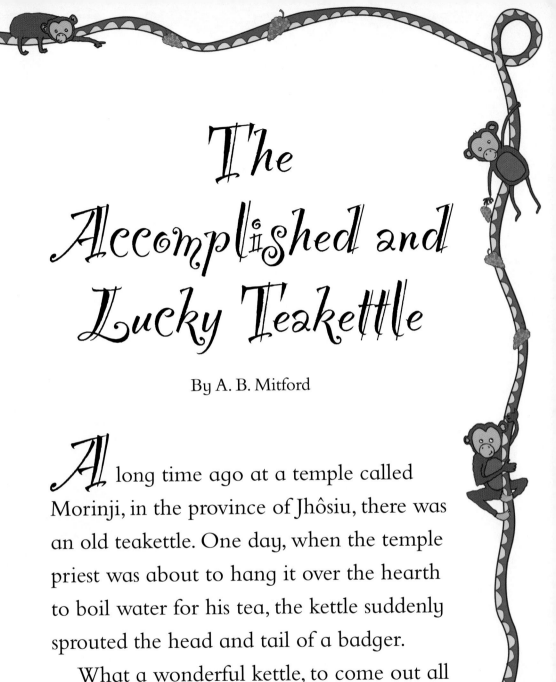

The Accomplished and Lucky Teakettle

By A. B. Mitford

A long time ago at a temple called Morinji, in the province of Jhôsiu, there was an old teakettle. One day, when the temple priest was about to hang it over the hearth to boil water for his tea, the kettle suddenly sprouted the head and tail of a badger.

What a wonderful kettle, to come out all over with fur!

The Accomplished and Lucky Teakettle

The priest, thunderstruck, called in the youngest monks of the temple to see the sight. While they were stupidly staring, one suggesting one thing and another another thing, the kettle jumped up into the air and began flying around the room. More astonished than ever, the priest and his pupils tried to chase it, but no thief or cat was ever half so sharp as this wonderful badger-kettle.

At last, however, they managed to knock it down and secure it. Holding it in with their joint efforts, they forced it into a box, intending to carry it off and throw it away in some distant place, so that they might be no more plagued by the goblin. For this day their troubles were over, but, as luck would have it, the tinker who was in the habit of working for the temple called in. The priest suddenly thought that it was a pity to throw the kettle away for nothing, and he might as well get a small amount for it, no matter how tiny.

33

So he brought out the kettle, which had gone back to its former shape, and showed it to the tinker. When the tinker saw the kettle, he offered twenty copper coins for it, and the priest was only too glad to close the bargain and be rid of the troublesome piece. The tinker trudged off home with his new purchase.

That night, as the tinker lay asleep, he heard a strange noise near his pillow. He peered out from under the bedclothes, and there he saw the kettle covered with fur and walking about on four legs. The tinker started up in a fright to see what it could all mean, when all of a sudden the kettle went back to its former shape. This happened over and over again, until at last the tinker

showed the teakettle to a friend, who said:
"This is certainly an accomplished and
lucky teakettle. You should take it around
as a show, with songs and music, and make
it dance and walk on the tightrope."

The Accomplished and Lucky Teakettle

The tinker, thinking this good advice, made arrangements with a showman, and set up an exhibition. The noise of the kettle's performances soon spread abroad. Even the Princes of the land sent to order the tinker to come to them, and he grew rich beyond all his expectations. Even the Princesses, too, and the great ladies of the court, took great delight in the dancing kettle, so that no sooner had it shown its tricks in one place than it was time for them to keep some other engagement.

At last the tinker grew so rich that he took the kettle back to the temple, where it was laid up as a precious treasure, and worshiped as a saint.

Bruin and Reynard

By Sir George Webbe Dasent

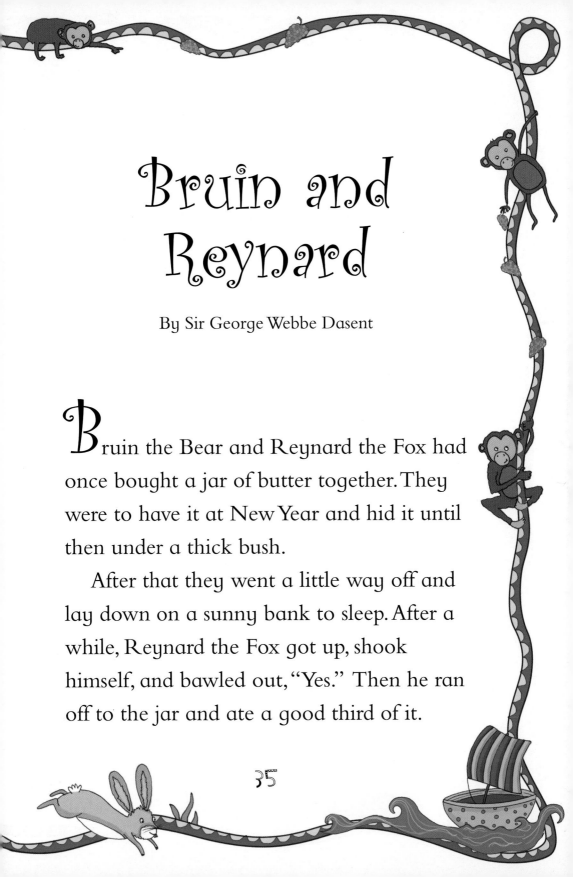

Bruin the Bear and Reynard the Fox had once bought a jar of butter together. They were to have it at New Year and hid it until then under a thick bush.

After that they went a little way off and lay down on a sunny bank to sleep. After a while, Reynard the Fox got up, shook himself, and bawled out, "Yes." Then he ran off to the jar and ate a good third of it.

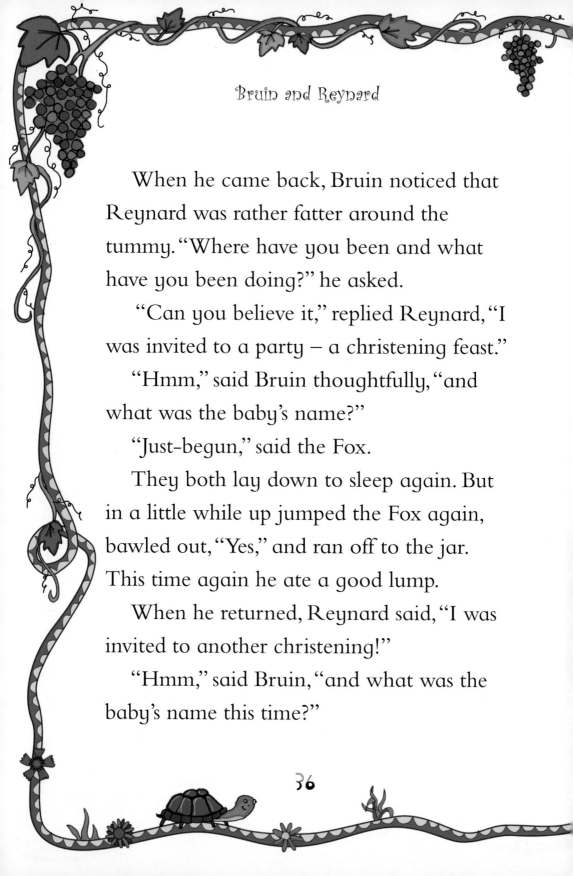

When he came back, Bruin noticed that Reynard was rather fatter around the tummy. "Where have you been and what have you been doing?" he asked.

"Can you believe it," replied Reynard, "I was invited to a party – a christening feast."

"Hmm," said Bruin thoughtfully, "and what was the baby's name?"

"Just-begun," said the Fox.

They both lay down to sleep again. But in a little while up jumped the Fox again, bawled out, "Yes," and ran off to the jar. This time again he ate a good lump.

When he returned, Reynard said, "I was invited to another christening!"

"Hmm," said Bruin, "and what was the baby's name this time?"

"Half-eaten," said Reynard.

Bruin thought that a very strange name, but before he had wondered long over it, he began to yawn, and he fell asleep.

Bruin hadn't lain long before Reynard the Fox jumped up again, bawled out, "Yes," and ran off to the jar, which this time he finished right off. When he got back he

told Bruin that he had been invited to yet
another christening. When the Bear wanted
to know the baby's name, he answered,
"All-gone."

    After that they laid down again,
and slept for a long time. Then
they got up to go to the

jar of butter. When they found it eaten, each said one had been at the jar while the other slept.

"We'll soon find this out," said Reynard. "We'll lay in the sun, and he whose cheeks are greasiest when we wake, he is the thief."

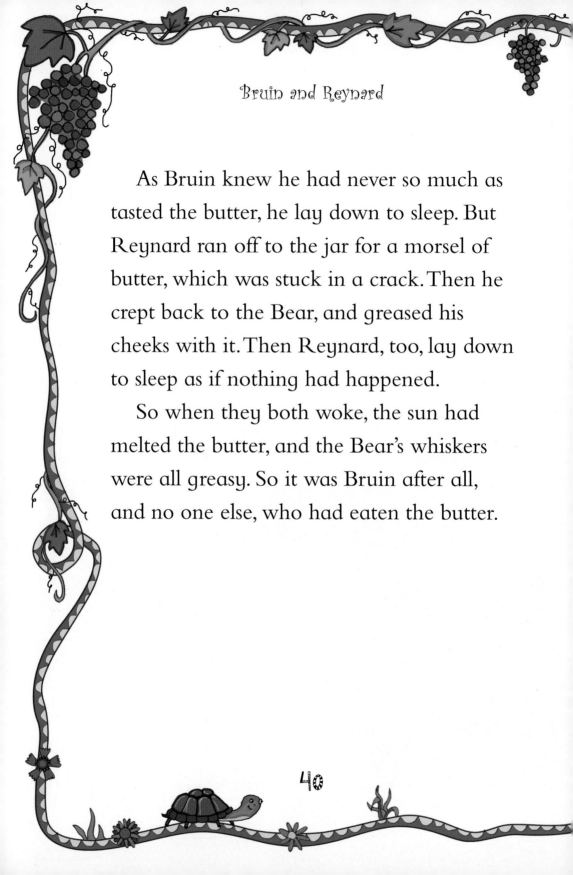

Bruin and Reynard

As Bruin knew he had never so much as tasted the butter, he lay down to sleep. But Reynard ran off to the jar for a morsel of butter, which was stuck in a crack. Then he crept back to the Bear, and greased his cheeks with it. Then Reynard, too, lay down to sleep as if nothing had happened.

So when they both woke, the sun had melted the butter, and the Bear's whiskers were all greasy. So it was Bruin after all, and no one else, who had eaten the butter.